A CHRISTMAS RIDESHARE

LILY DAE

PHONE

*M*om: *I can't wait to finally meet Roxanne! Does she have any food allergies? Love, Bunny*

Mom: What size sweater does she wear? I hope I got the right size. We'll have to take the Ugly Sweater photo right when you two arrive if we're going to use it for the invitations. Love, Bunny

Mom: Aunt Janice is here! She says to send a selfie. No one knows what you look like anymore! Love, Bunny

Mom: I said that last part. Love, Bunny

CHARLOTTE

I turned off my oversized phone and pocketed it. There were sweaty, mustached men in my apartment packing up my life.

"You're taking the kitchen table?" My voice was more of a squeak than an actual, adult human sound. The movers shot each other a not-again look as they wrapped the dining table in a moving quilt.

"Yeah, I paid for it," Roxanne said as another mover slid a naked mattress down the hall.

"And, the mattress?"

"Yeah."

She was so matter-of-fact scrolling through her phone like it was just any other day.

"What's going on, Rex? Why are you doing this?" The words fell heavily from my mouth. They felt like work. When she didn't even look up from her phone, they turned to molten lava.

"Specifically," I said, slapping my hand over her screen, "why are you doing this now?"

Now. Why now? We were less than 24 hours away from

our first official Christmas together as a couple. My parents bought her an ugly sweater for our annual Ugly Sweater Party. We'd been living together for six months, I thought we might actually, god, this sounds so stupid - I actually thought we were going to get engaged soon.

"We just want different things."

"Since yesterday?!" She slid her phone into her back pocket and walked over to the half-wall that divided the dining area from the kitchen in our small apartment.

I watched her unplug the Alexa and wrap the cord around her hand. She leaned in and kissed my forehead while cradling our...her Alexa in the crook of her arm.

"You're really doing this?"

"Yeah," she said without hesitation. She turned and walked toward the door without looking back or anything. She just closed the door.

I looked around at my barren apartment. All that was left was an empty TV stand, my bookshelf, and reading chair.

"Where the fuck am I supposed to sleep?!"

CHARLOTTE

I had only just told my folks about Roxanne. It was all so good and still had that new relationship smell to it. I didn't want to jinx it. This is what I get for blabbing. A bowl of cereal for dinner and a vintage reading chair for a bed.

I kicked my feet up on the empty entertainment center. Just as I was about to take a bite, my phone vibrated and chimed.

Ding.

A blurry photo of mom and Aunt Janice appeared. Someone's finger, most likely dad's, was in the corner, and the two of them were holding goldfish bowl-sized wine glasses filled to the brim with what I imagine was white wine and lots of ice.

I had been single for so long. "Single Charlotte." Every holiday, baby shower, and family gathering, someone would make a fuss that "Single Charlotte" had arrived… alone…again.

I wasn't against relationships as a rule! I had been swamped since I was two years old. Jazz, tap, spelling bees.

You name it; I did it! Adventure camps, science camps, run club, and 4H in elementary school and junior high.

Then, I focused on high school. High GPA. Extracurriculars. Then, college. Bachelor's in Business. Graduated early. Got a good job, and then I got a great job.

The great job came with benefits. Those benefits were flirtatious sticky notes at first. Then, late-night meetings. Then, dinner. And, then well, then a small apartment recently emptied by large men with impressive mustaches. A missing cylindrical device that told those who gathered around it what the weather was going to be for the weekend. Cereal for dinner. And, in Tennessee, a family waiting to admit a new member…finally.

Me: Don't start the party without me!

Mom: We're saving the good stuff for you and my future daughter-in-law, darling! Don't worry! Love, Bunny

Me: About that - I'll be coming alon-

I'll be coming alone. I could have just told them I was coming alone, and that I did not want to talk about it. Right? Right.

Mom: We are just thrilled, darling! I am so happy you've finally found someone. What a wonderful Christmas gift for the family! Love, Bunny

Well, shit.

CHARLOTTE

*T*he flight from Chicago to Nashville is short. Only about two hours, and while it is nice to fly with an empty seat beside you, it makes the flight longer knowing who was supposed to be sitting there.

What was I going to tell my parents and Aunt Janice? I could straight-up lie and say something like, "Oh, I lost Rex on the flight! Silly me! I'd lose my head if it weren't attached!"

No way that would work.

I could just stay on the plane. I could just stay on the plane and go back and forth from the airport to the airport. Planes are subways, right? I could just keep flying.

Telling the truth wasn't going to make this trip any better. I couldn't take a week of my mother looking disappointed and the neighbors frowning at me while saying backhanded sympathetic platitudes, "Well, Charlotte, this is an opportunity to get to know yourself. You have to love yourself before you can love someone else." As if I don't have a clue who I am! As if I don't think I am worthy of a relationship.

I felt my chest start to tighten, and my breaths were

getting shorter and shorter. I had to stop telling myself stories like this, but I knew that was what it would be like.

The truth is that I do actually love myself, anxiety, and all. I think my life is worth sharing with someone, but I wanted to make sure I was sharing my life with someone worth it. So, yes, I dragged my feet a little. A lot. I met Rex and thought she was worth it, but...

More tightness and shorter breaths were coming on.

"Ma'am. Would you like some water? Or a paper bag?" A woman with a tightly wrapped bun leaned over my seat with a small water bottle in hand.

"Thank you," I whispered, taking the water.

"There's an airsickness bag in the pocket of the seat in front of you. Please press the flight attendant button if you need anything."

I turned pink with embarrassment. "Thank you." The other few passengers on the flight gave me sideways glances as I fanned myself with the paper bag and sipped my little water.

Only a few moments after, we were all jarred slightly as the plane landed at BNA. Time to face the music.

It was unseasonably cold. Nashville is known for its fickle weather, and we were receiving that fickleness in full. It was sixty degrees when I checked the weather before I left my apartment. And, of course, the temperature dropped the moment I left Chicago. I was standing in the 34-degree cold in ripped jeans and a fashionable but breezy cashmere sweater.

I opened the Tag-A-Ride app and chose the ride closest to me. Headlights on a large, black SUV flashed the moment I scanned my thumbprint.

Please, let there be heat in there!

OPAL

"Take the first fare that comes your way," I said to my reflection in the rearview mirror. "This doesn't have to be a long night at all. One quick pick-up and drop-off, and you can go home, have some tea, and read a book. And, you know what, you don't have to do this ever again."

I knew I could rely on a quick fare from BNA. Tourism in the city was always high, but around the holidays, drivers were overwhelmed with requests.

The moment I turned on my Tag-A-Ride, my phone began vibrating and chirping. A bubble appeared on the screen with a picture of a blonde girl in pale pink aviators.

"PinkCupcake tagged you," said the Tag-A-Ride AI voice.

I flashed my headlights and tapped the "You're it!" bubble to confirm the ride. I saw a blur of blonde hair and pink fuzz heading my direction. I could tell she was a talker. I took a deep breath, counted down from five, and unlocked the door.

CHARLOTTE

"*T*hank god!" A wave of warmth hugged me as I pulled opened the passenger door.

"Need help with your bags?" The driver asked, unbuckling her seatbelt.

"No, thanks. I'm good."

I would say I tossed my bags in the backseat with a wild abandon, but that would be an understatement. The skin showing through my jeans was turning blue!

"Do you mind if I sit in the front?" I shouted from the floorboard, where I was stowing my carry-on.

"Sit wherever you like, ma'am."

"Ma'am? You don't have to call me ma'am." I whipped the back door closed, opened the passenger door, and hopped onto the step rail. A hand extended out to you me.

"Need some help up?"

She had a pleasant voice. A little smoky which suited her 80's Joan Jett look.

"Thank you. Point those bad boys at me!" I tilted all but one of the vents right at my thighs, letting the heat hit my skin through the rips.

9

"Nice jeans." She said softly as she adjusted the heat and turned on my seat warmer.

"I know I look ridiculous in this weather, but it was warm here when I got on the plane." I have no idea why I was getting defensive and sensitive about a compliment from a total stranger. I should have said thank you, but I just kept blabbing about the weather.

"They're supposed to be fashionable," the driver said, glancing at my jeans and shifting the SUV into drive, "but they're really just air conditioning that you can't control. Seat belt, please."

I didn't know what exactly I was supposed to say to that, so I reached over my shoulder, shot her a little side-eye, and belted myself in.

CHARLOTTE

M e: Landed. Headed your way.

Mom: Did you rent a car? I hope you two aren't riding with some stranger. Love, Mom

Mom: What kind of car did you get? Are you texting and driving? Love, Mom

Me: Got a Tag-a-Ride. Will be there soon.

I closed the messenger app and opened a browser.

Search: How to be an effective liar

Delete.

Search: How to convince people your girlfriend is invisible

Delete.

Time to bite the bullet. I was just going to tell them I came alone. My relationship, turns out, was not as stable as I thought, and I'm going to die alone most likely eaten by my neighbors' cats.

I started typing that last bit but immediately thought better of it. My shoulders sagged. I leaned back and looked out the window while wet sat on the edges of my eyelids.

"Warming up?" The Tag-A-Ride driver asked softly.

"Yeah. Thank you."

She lifted the corner of her mouth and nodded.

I opened my camera app to make sure I didn't look ridiculous - you know, like a grown woman crying in a strangers car because she doesn't want her mommy and daddy to find out she's been rejected.

She glanced over as I was wiping beneath my eye. The corner of her mouth lifted again. It would have made a great picture...

It would have made a great picture!

I had a plan. I wiggled in my seat a bit and lifted the phone.

I framed myself for a selfie and got the driver's head right over my shoulder, but she was like freaking Bigfoot! Always blurry and never even giving as much as profile shot!

Time to take it to the next level.

OPAL

$\mathcal{I}$ could see her fidgeting in my peripheral vision. She was about the change the destination last minute or ask to be dropped at a bathroom. I could tell.

"Hey, so this is going to sound strange, but can I take a picture of you?"

"Me?" That's a new one.

"Yeah."

"While I'm driving?"

"Yeah."

"Why?"

"Proof of life. For my mom."

"For your mom? How old are you?"

"Twenty-six. I'll give you twenty bucks."

"What are you going to do with it?"

"Send it to my mom. Then, I'll delete it. I promise."

She turned slightly in her seat and leaned her head back, almost resting on my shoulder. I suddenly smelled vanilla. An artificial shutter sound clicked before I could say anything else.

"Okay. One more, but this time can you smile?"

"I'm kind of driving right now."

"You can't smile and drive?"

"Point taken." I complied, and she snapped another.

"Not bad. Okay. We're going to nail it this time! Could you just..."

"Nope." I turned on the hazards and pulled over. Cars raced passed my door as I pulled to the shoulder of the highway.

"Okay. Who do you work for?" I was exhausted by the media. I didn't care how cute she was or what kind of baked goods she smelled like, I was going to have her fired.

"What?" "Are you a reporter? A blogger? A vlogger?"

She scrunched her face and looked genuinely confused. "What?"

"Okay. You can get out here."

"Here? On the interstate?!"

"I'll wait here with you until another Tag-A-Ride comes for you. Now, will you please delete that picture?"

"Excuse me, I'm paying for a ride, and I paid for that picture. I'm sending it."

"No transaction has taken place, and I did not agree to be photographed."

"I'll pay you once I get to my destination." Red crept up her neck and cheeks. I saw her jaw clench. I reached for my phone and swiped through the app.

"There's another car fifteen minutes from here. I'll take you to the gas station off the exit."

"Fine."

"Delete the pictures."

CHARLOTTE

Two minutes later, we were sitting in the parking lot of a truck stop. She tapped on her phone a few times and slouched hard in the driver's seat.

"I'm sorry. I know that was weird. If you will just hear me out before you send for that other car. I think we can help each other out here."

"I'm really not in the mood. The ride is on me. Both of them."

"Please, hear me out. It's Christmas."

An audible sigh followed by a frustrated groan bounced around the interior of the SUV. She placed the phone down on the dash. "I'm listening."

"First, no. I'm not a blogger or anything."

"Go on."

"I can't believe I'm telling my rideshare driver this, but I was dumped yesterday. She took my fucking mattress." The words were escaping before I could form a coherent storyline. "My family is expecting my very serious girlfriend for an ugly sweater party and me."

Her eyebrows furrowed. "Well, I have so many questions."

"Look, here's what I'm thinking. You take this photo with me and pretend to be Rex. Roxanne. We go to my folks' place, you pose for our ugly sweater photo, and then you get an "emergency text," and have to leave. No one will ever know. It will be our secret for life. I'll take this one to the grave if you just save me this humiliation and another year of my mom asking me for grandchildren!"

"And how does this benefit me?"

"I'll give you five stars?"

She crossed her arms and screwed the corners of her mouth.

"And I'll pay you! No one drives during the holidays if they aren't looking for extra cash. I can throw some your way. I'm not rich or anything, but I can invest a few dollars in a peaceful holiday vacation with my family."

"How much?"

"Fifty. And, and I'll feed you!" She took a deep breath and leaned on the steering wheel.

"Please? I can't tell my parents my first real relationship has ended without any good reason.

She leaned her head back and sighed. Her finger curled over pursed lips. She was either genuinely considering it or wondering how good a shot she had of just making a run for it.

After a moment of tense silence, she pinched between her eyebrows, closed her eyes, and said, "How long have we been together?"

Lightning energy whipped through my body.

"Nine months, but we've known each other for about a year."

"How did we meet?"

"At work."

"Ew, that's going to be uncomfortable when you get back."

"Tell me about it." I slumped.

She adjusted herself in the driver's seat and flitted her lapels. "Okay. Let's do this."

My eyebrows went rogue. "Really?"

"Yeah." She unbuckled her seat belt and slid toward the center console. Her right arm reached for the headrest behind me. I leaned into the crook of her arm, resting my head on her shoulder.

"You're a saint! You are not going to regret this. There is so much good karma coming to you for this!"

"Uh huh. Let's do this."

I snapped a perfectly ordinary photo of two strangers pretending to be in love.

"This is great!"

"How long will you be reserving me?"

"Twenty minutes at my folks' place. Tops!"

"I can't believe I'm doing this…" She mumbled as she shifted into drive and put us back on the road.

PHONE

*M*e: *I had to pee. Almost there!*

      Mom: *Must you always tell me when you are in the bathroom? Is that her? She's quite Gothic looking. I do love a classic shag haircut. Love, Bunny.*

CHARLOTTE

*S*he was rather dark. We looked like the perfect picture of good and evil in our fraudulent selfie with my soft pink sweater and pale blonde hair against her black hair, black shirt, and black scarf.

"What's my name again?" She asked, pulling me out of my examination of her clothing.

"Roxanne, but I call you Rex."

"Like T-Rex?"

"Yeah."

"What do I do for a living?"

"You're the director of marketing at the publishing house."

"Director of marketing. How old am I supposed to be?"

"Thirty. How old are you?"

"Thirty-two. Anything else I need to know before we get to your folks' house?"

"Nah. I didn't really tell them too much."

"Because you weren't sure about the relationship?"

"Excuse me?" I said immediately defensive of my recently broken relationship.

"I didn't mean to offend. It just seems like if you were sure about the relationship you would have, I don't know, talked about your girlfriend. Sent a picture."

"Ooh! Turn here. It's this house on the left. Park anywhere."

I hoped my rapid change of topic was enough of a hint in the direction of this-is-none-of-your-business.

We pulled onto the herringbone-patterned driveway. I had that nervous feeling in my gut like I had been out past curfew for eleven months.

"So, my name is Roxanne. We met at work, and we've been together for about nine months."

I nodded in confirmation. "Yep."

"Where's your coat?" She cracked the door letting the cold, night air blow in.

"In Chicago. I thought it was supposed to be warm for the next few days. Oofah!" Her heavy wool coat landed in my lap.

"No, no. I don't need it." "I'm not letting you walk outside in this," she gestured to the flurries that had started only a second earlier, "in those would-be jeans and that suggestion of a sweater. You'll freeze."

"It's really okay."

"Do you want your parents to think your girlfriend doesn't care about you enough to make sure you're warm? Take the damn coat. I'll get the bags." She closed the door, and then immediately reopened it, "Hey, what do I call you?"

"Oh, my god! I never told you my name. I'm Charlotte. Charlotte Greene with an E." I extended my hand.

"Opal Blakewood." She reached in and shook my hand hard. "Start your timer, Charlotte. You've got twenty minutes."

CHARLOTTE

*T*he decorations on the house were tasteful and not at all overboard. Large velvet ribbons were tied on the antique door knockers, and simple wreaths were on every window. My mom, Bunny, as she liked to be called, loved things neat and tidy. They have to be considering how wild and chaotic her mind is.

"Nice digs."

"Thanks."

"Did you grow up here?"

"Yep."

"Must have been quite a childhood."

"Whatever you're thinking it was, you're probably right. Just make sure you sprinkle some social pressure on all of that cotton candy."

"Right." She chuckled and nodded.

"Jesus, Opal. I can't thank you enough."

"Yes, you can. With many sandwiches."

"No problem. I'll throw in a good bottle of wine too."

"Hey, now." She half-smiled.

I reached out to ring the doorbell when I noticed she was still two feet behind me.

"Come here." I grabbed her arm and draped it over my shoulder. "Sell it."

I pressed the doorbell.

"You ring the doorbell at your own house?" she whispered.

"This is my mother's house, so yes."

"Oh, they're here! They're here," sang a voice from behind the door.

"Brace yourself, Roxanne." I said, waggling my eyebrows. Both doors flew open.

"Darling!" Chanel filled the air as she wrapped her arms around us both. "Roxanne. May I call you Roxanne? You are just delightfully monochromatic." She held Opal's arms outstretched and observed her black, silk button down and black, wool scarf. "Charlotte, take these bags, dear." Bunny took the bags from Opal and sat them on the small porch. "I do love a solid, single-color ensemble. You must come in." She opened her plaid poncho and wrapped a wing around her shoulder, guiding her toward the door. "It's dreadfully cold out. Oh!" She turned to look at me, "Aunt Janice is staying in the guest room," She clasped my face in her hands, "You and Roxanne will take your old room, and dad and I will take our room, of course! Come, come. Get out of this freezing cold, child." She wrapped her arm in Opal's. "Darling, do tell us all how you manage ever to get a word in edgewise with this one. She inherited the gift of gab from her father. Oh! Lewis! You're only daughter has arrived with her lady love, and you're still watching the game?!"

"I'm not sleeping. I'm resting my eyes." His voice carried from the overstuffed, reading chair.

"Mom." I stepped inside and closed the door on the cold,

"Mom. Bunny!" I grabbed her arm and spun her toward me. "Yes, darling."

"How about Roxanne and I drop off our luggage, and you get everyone together for the ugly sweater photo?"

"Splendid idea, darling. Your sweaters are on the bed." She squeezed my arms before marching toward the living room, continuing to talk to all available ears. "Change quickly, so we can start the festivities! Lewis! Get the camera, love!"

I took a deep breath and turned toward Opal, who was standing with her mouth agape and eyes unblinking.

"Breathe."

"Wow," she said.

"Yeah. That's mom or Bunny."

"Wow. Is that Mid-Atlantic? Is she from a Michael Curtiz film?"

"Come with me. We can get sweatered up and get you out of here. If we move at Bunny's speed, we can have you out of here in ten minutes."

"Magic."

OPAL

The Greenes were well off. Large home in an expensive neighborhood. Old money for sure.

Old money is different from new money. It smells different. It looks different.

Bunny was old money with her strawberry hair and gold jewelry. The house was vintage as well. As we walked up the curved staircase, I noticed oil paintings and family portraits alike in gilded frames.

"It's this one here." Charlotte nodded in the direction of a door with a wooden sign that said CHARLOTTE in a serif font.

"Are you sure?"

"Careful with that sarcasm. You'll chip away at all of that good karma you're earning."

The room was immaculate. Rose wallpaper and a deep walnut mid-wall trim. The furniture looked antique.

"Where do you want these?" I held up the suitcase and overnight bag.

"Just drop them anywhere." She kicked off her shoes.

"Let's get these sweaters on." She held up a large blue sweater with …

"Are those..?"

"3-D antlers? Oh, yeah." She tossed it to me.

"It looks a little small."

"Rex is shorter than you are," she felt around my waist. I immediately put my hands up like I was under arrest. "But you're thinner in the middle. It should work out. I'll change in the bathroom. You can change out here."

CHARLOTTE

"*T*his is not a problem. In and out in ten minutes. We can do this."

I developed the habit of talking to myself in the mirror when I was a teenager. My reflection helped me through exams, barrel races, prom, and every single holiday since I moved out.

"Nobody suspects a thing. Just be cool. You got this." I high-fived myself and walked out of the bathroom and saw Opal slide the ridiculous sweater over her head.

"The neck of this thing is really small." Her words were muffled against the fabric. Her back was to me, and I noticed some calligraphy on her shoulder before I saw the flailing of her arms. I couldn't contain myself.

"I'm gonna pee!" I doubled over with tears in my eyes. "I'm gonna pee!"

"I'm so glad you're enjoying yourself."

"I am! I really am!" I fell to my knees, trying to hold back the laughter.

"That's it." She whipped the sweater off and turned

around. "I'm going to have to stretch the neck of this thing if you want me to wear it, okay?"

I collected myself, stood up, and straightened the antlers on my sweater — all business. We locked eyes. Opal's shoulders began to quake, and she held her lips shut. And, then, she lost it.

"This is…the most… ridiculous…" She doubled over and couldn't even get all of the words out.

"I know! I know! Here. Let me help." I said, wiping tears away from my eyes.

She doubled over, holding the sweater out. She took a deep breath and stood upright.

"Wow. You're …tall." I had to tilt my head up to meet her gaze.

"I'm just still wearing my shoes."

"Oh. Right." I stretched the neck of the sweater in little sections glancing at Opal's arms. Her chest had actual muscle striations. She was wearing a thin, spaghetti-strapped tank top: the kind that only looks good the mannequin.

I didn't mean to gawk, but Roxanne, while athletic, wasn't built anything like this.

"CrossFit." Opal said.

OPAL

"*H*uh?"

"I do CrossFit," I said, looking down at her.

"Oh, I wasn't looking. Here you go." She whipped her head around, turning her back to me.

"Knock, knock!" Bunny doesn't open doors. She flings them. "Everybody decent?"

I yanked the shirt over my head and down as far as it would go. It just met my belt line.

"Oh, sorry to startle you, dear! Don't you look just fantastic! Roxanne, darling, straighten your antlers. They're a little droopy." Bunny took an antler in each hand and moved there here and there.

I chuckled to myself while Charlotte hung her head in embarrassment.

"It's picture time, darlings! Shoes optional!"

Bunny clapped her hands and spun on her heels.

"That woman is a tornado."

"You have no idea."

CHARLOTTE

*W*e descended the staircase in our antler sweaters. As we round the curve, I heard a warm, familiar voice.

"Happy Christmas Time!"

"Aunt Janice!"

"Charlotte, sweetheart!" She gave my hands a comforting squeeze. "This must be the famous Roxanne. I understand you like to be called Rex, is that right?"

"Whatever is easiest for you, ma'am."

"Ma'am? Such insulting manners. Call me Janice."

"Honey," I slid my arm around Opal, "I've told you about my famous Aunt Janice. She's the travel photographer who took all of those pictures in our bedroom. The glaciers." I was pleading as much as one person could with their eyes.

"Oh, of course. Great, great photos. I love a good glacier."

"Oh, me too. Have you ever seen any in person?"

"Actually-" she started. "Hey, Aunt Janice. I think mom needs your help with the timer on the camera."

"Lewis can handle it. It's my night off. You were saying, Rex?"

I squeezed Opal's hip using what I hoped was morse code for, "Abort! Make a run for the door!" "Actually," she squeezed my shoulder as she spoke, "I hiked Falljökull a couple of years ago."

"No! I'm going there next year! How was it?"

"Yeah. It was a life-changing experience."

"Did you take many pictures while you were hiking?"

"Unfortunately, I didn't get many. I was traveling with a group, but I was there alone, so…you know how that goes. But, I'd love to go back before they change too much or worse."

"You two should come with me. I can be your unofficial vacation photographer! What do ya say?"

"Oh, let's not plan too far ahead there, Aunt Janice." An awkward silence fell between us, and then there was Bunny.

"We're ready!"

What followed was our standard family Christmas photo shoot. Mom and Dad. Mom and dad kissing under the mistletoe. Just mom. Just dad. Mom and Janice. Just mom again. Dad and Janice. Just Janice.

"Girls! You're up!" Bunny shouted. We stood by the fireplace she with her hands in her pockets and me with my hands folded in front of me.

"That's lovely, girls. Now, pretend to like each other." Aunt Janice said with a giggle. I slid my arm around her waist again. She was just tall enough. We fit like puzzle pieces. She put her arm around my shoulder.

"Smile!" Bunny shouted.

"I thought this was a group photo," Opal whispered through clenched teeth.

"It is. We just have to get through this part first." I said.

"Wonderful, darlings!" Bunny clasped her hands in front of her heart, gleefully.

"Okay, group shot!" I shouted.

"Darling…" Bunny pointed toward the ceiling. Opal and I looked up.

"Oh." We said, eyeing the mistletoe.

"Oh, I don't think that's appropriate," I said.

"A tiny Christmas kiss for a photo isn't vulgar!" Bunny said, placing her hands on her hips.

"Will you kiss my cheek, please?" I pleaded through a toothy grin.

"This is harassment." She murmured.

"Please?"

"It will cost you extra." She said, leaning toward me.

"Name it." My whisper-scream was getting pretty good. Her lips brushed against my ear.

"I'm keeping this awful sweater." I covered my mouth to keep from laughing, and I felt soft, warm lips on my cheek.

OPAL

"Aww." Bunny said as Aunt Janice snapped away.

After I made the Tag-A-Ride app, my life changed. At first, all of the changes were positive. I had money - enough to send some back to my family, a girlfriend that I loved, and a bright future ahead of me.

My girlfriend became my wife, and my parents didn't approve. They didn't trust her, and they were right to have withheld their trust.

"Okay, okay," Charlotte announced, "let's group photo now, please. Thank you."

After the group photos, we scattered. Lewis, who doesn't talk very much, sat in his chair and watched whatever sport was on, Aunt Janice and Bunny had what I imagined was their third bottle of white wine for the day, and Charlotte and I went to the kitchen so I could collect my payment.

"You are a saint. If I could give you this whole refrigerator, I would."

"A sandwich will do."

"And that bottle of wine?"

"Oh, I couldn't impose like that."

"It's not a problem at all. Are you a red or white?"

"Either would be wonderful."

She raised a stern eyebrow at me and pulled on a cabinet door that slid out and revealed a wine rack that was full of beautiful wine bottles.

"Thank you for the offer, but I really can't take your parents' wine."

"It's our wine. We make it. There's plenty more in the cellar."

"Well, in that case." She slid the bottle over to me.

"Greene Acres Wine. Cute."

"I know you have to go, but do you want to stay for a glass? You earned it out there. They loved you!" She was smiling with her eyes. I always envied people who were happy and free enough to do that kind of thing.

"I won't lie that sounds tempting, but it's definitely been more than 20 minutes. I should really go. The longer I'm here, the more obvious it will become that I'm not," I covered my mouth to conceal the secret, "A t-rex."

"Sure. Sure."

She made a couple of sandwiches and hid them in my coat pockets. She walked me to the living room with her hand under my coat to conceal the wine bottle behind my back.

"Hey, guys. Rex has to go back to Chicago. Big work emergency, so she's leaving now. Say bye. Bye! Okay, good!"

"No," they whined, "We were so looking forward to spending some more time with you."

"Yeah, I was too." I said, folding down the corners of my mouth.

"She has to leave right now if she's going to make her flight. Okay? Okay. Bye." She opened the door, and that's when we saw it.

CHARLOTTE

"*O*h, no," Opal said.

"Shit. Shit. Shit." I squeezed the life out of the wine bottle.

"So…"

"We can fix this," I said.

Opal turned to me slowly, and whisper-shouted, "It's snow. How do you fix snow?!"

"I don't know!" I whisper-shouted back.

"How long were we in there? What time is it?"

"Shit…it's 10:30."

"I was in there for two hours?"

"Well, look at that. Bunny, you got your wish." Dad stood between us, holding a giant sandwich.

CHARLOTTE

"Can you believe this weather?" Aunt Janice pulled up a barstool and raised her glass.

"Here's to global warming, ladies."

"Oh, stop it with that nonsense." Bunny waved her hands in a fit.

"So," I said, spreading the Rudolph placemat over the marble countertop. "Roxanne is new…"

"Oh, we aren't fighting, dear. Aunt Janice here is just a believer in doom and gloom."

Aunt Janice leaned into Opal, "That means 'facts.' I am a supporter of facts."

"We've had 60-degree weather three Christmases in a row. Fact. And yet, here we sit on the eve of Christmas Eve snowed in. What more evidence do you need?"

"Climate change is not the weather!"

"Oh, god. Please, stop. Please, stop. Please, stop." I could feel my cheeks turning red. My head got heavier and heavier.

"Facts are facts. No one is disputing that, dear sister. The fact is there is snow falling from the sky, and I prayed for it. Climate change isn't real, and prayer works. End of story."

They loved this. Aunt Janice and Bunny spent their entire childhoods doing this. Challenging each other.

I leapt to my feet. "We're going to bed now! Goodnight!"

"Why?" Aunt Janice whined, "We were just getting started."

"You two realize this kind of banter is only fun for you, right?"

"It is fun for all who wish to participate." Bunny leaned over the counter conspiratorially, "Roxanne, darling," she folded her fingers, "do you believe in God?"

"Wow, mom…"

"Bunny." She raised an eyebrow at me. "Bunny, this is wildly inappropriate."

"If God is a fact," Opal clipped, cutting against the end of my sentence, "then my belief in God is irrelevant, Mrs. Greene. All that really matters is how much God is willing to believe in me."

Bunny's eyes were fixed on the fake Roxanne, then she looked at me, and the edges of her mouth curled up.

"Marry her, darling. I officially like her more than I like either of you," she said, smiling and waggling her finger between Aunt Janice and me.

OPAL

"Goodnight." She said as she closed and locked the bedroom door.

"Am I a prisoner?" I joked.

"No, but we don't want anyone coming in and seeing us not sleeping together."

"Understood. About that, I can probably make it out of here."

"Do you have all-weather tires on that luxury vehicle of yours?"

"Umm, no."

"Where did you live before here?" "Arizona."

"Ever driven in snow before?"

"Can't say that I have. Not a lot of snow anyway. Not like this. But it's still fresh. Surely, the roads haven't gotten slick yet."

"It isn't about the roads. It's about the drivers that think the roads are slick. Yeah, you're staying here."

She shoved off the edge of the bed and rummaged through a giant closet, eventually pulling out a pale pink, knitted blanket, and a pillow.

"I'll take the floor," I said, taking the pillow and blanket from her.

"Absolutely not. You would be home right now if it weren't for me. I deserve the floor."

"It's really okay."

"Oh, my god! I didn't even think to ask! Is your family waiting for you? Pets? Do you need to call anyone, and let them know you're safe?"

"I had no plans tonight. I'm good."

"What about clothes? You can't sleep in that." She started to accelerate, "I'm a little short compared to you, but I have big t-shirts and sweats. Or maybe some shorts. I can get my dad's pj pants…"

"Whoa, whoa, whoa…Take a beat." I sat down the blanket and pillow, "Let's just forget about everything for a second and breathe, shall we?"

I offered her my hands, and she took them. I bowed my head and took a long, deep breath followed by a loud audible sigh. I could feel her eyes on me.

"Just try it," I said. We stood there with our heads bowed, holding each other's hands breathing loud sighs at the floor.

"Thank you," she sighed. "I don't mean to be nosey, but do you have anxiety?"

"Only when things are stressful."

"How often are things stressful?"

"You met Bunny."

"Okay. I have a suggestion just to get us through the night. You tell me what you think of it, and we'll go from there. How does that sound?"

"Sounds good." Her eyes were like saucers. She nodded and crossed her arms.

"I'll take care of me…"

"Yes. Uh, huh." She kept nodding.

"And, you take care of you."

"Yes."

I let the idea hang in the air. She looked like she was waiting for more, but there wasn't anything more to say. Not from me. The nodding slowed, and it was settled.

"Okay." She said, releasing her arms.

"Okay." I said. I stepped aside to let her pass.

We were silent for the next few minutes. I sorted the blanket and pillow on the floor out of the way of the bathroom door and bed. I folded the quilt in a book-like fold.

I made my way downstairs, taking my coat and scarf from the thin, coat closet. The snow was thick and wet. Perfect for snowman building.

I reached my SUV and opened the back hatch my feet slide this way and that. My gym bag had a small shower kit inside. It wasn't an overnight bag, but at least, I'd have my own toothbrush.

When I came back into the room, Charlotte was standing in the bathroom doorway wearing giant glasses and baggy sleeping clothes. Her hair was tied into a messy bun, and she was staring at my makeshift bed. The whole picture was quite adorable.

"I thought you left," she said through a literal mouthful of foam. I held up my gym bag.

"I keep a toothbrush in my gym bag." She sighed and nodded. We danced between each other for a bit going from bathroom to bedroom.

After I had taken my turn in the bathroom, I came out to find her already tucked into bed, hugging her pillow. I tiptoed to my bed for the evening and settled.

"Good night, John Boy." She said.

"Good night, Jim Bob." I said through a toothy grin.

"Don't you just love The Waltons." She said sleepily.

"I really do."

CHARLOTTE

I stretched, rolled over on my side and snuggled with my pillow. I opened my eyes and caught a glimpse of a pile of person on my floor.

I had almost forgotten it all. The break-up, the Tag-A-Ride, and the kind stranger on the floor was saving my ass and working for sandwiches.

I pulled the blankets away and quietly went to the window. If the snow had let up, there was a good chance we could get Opal out of here.

When I opened the curtains, I was met with a scene from a Thomas Kinkade painting. The snow had fallen all night, and flurries were still dancing in the air. It was beautiful and calming for two seconds.

"Shit."

"Hey," said a sleepy voice from the floor.

"Hey. Did I wake you? I'm sorry." She chuckled.

"You've got to stop doing that?"

"Doing what?" "Asking a question and then apologizing before even hearing if you need to."

"I don't do that!" I put my fists on my hip in defiance. She propped herself up on her elbows.

"How does it look out there?"

"White."

"Really?"

"Yeah."

"That's pretty cool."

"Cool?"

"Yeah. I normally have to travel to see snow like this."

"I'm sorry to say it means you're stuck here."

"I still think I can get out of this," she pointed at the snow where the driveway used to be, "but I don't know if I can make it out of the neighborhood."

There was no way anyone was making it out of the neighborhood. The only way we were getting out of the house was with snow shovels, which no one in Tennessee owns.

"Darlings!" Bunny's voices echoed in the hall, and the clicking of her heels was getting louder. I turned to Opal, who had already sprung into action, rolling up her bedding and placing it on the floor of the closet.

"Your shirt!"

She looked down and shrugged her shoulders as if to say, "What about it?"

"Take it off!" I whisper shouted at her. She furrowed her brows and watched me as I unlocked the door and jumped back into bed. It all clicked, and a soft "oh" escaped her lips.

She yanked the black button down over her head, revealing her black, silk camisole. She jumped into bed beside me, and we hurriedly but wordlessly fit ourselves together. Her arm slid under my pillow, and I backed into her. She wrapped her arm around my waist, and I closed my eyes, hoping she'd done the same.

"Darlings! Oh!" Bunny's grand entrance into my bedroom was paused briefly as she took in the sight of me and my "girlfriend" sleeping. I heard, "Aw," followed immediately by zippy high heels clicks going back down the hall.

We sat up and looked around. The door was still open.

"Oh, no."

"What?" Opal whispered.

"Listen," I held my finger up in the air to shush her, "She's coming back!"

We tucked ourselves back in as I listened to footsteps that were coming closer, moving away, then coming closer. My heart was beating out of my chest. I could literally hear my blood flowing. I was starting to feel like I couldn't take a deep breath.

"Hey," her lips were butterfly wings on my ears. She gently pulled me in closer. "It's okay. Well, it's not exactly okay. It's hilarious, but it's still okay."

"Pfft!" I lost it. It was hilarious.

"I have essentially kidnapped you, made you pretend to be my girlfriend, and now we are playing opossum in my mom's house on Christmas Eve. You can't make this shit up!" Laughter erupted through the room as it could no longer be contained inside of us.

"Oh, no! I missed it!" She was hefting Aunt Janice's 50-pound camera.

"Good morning to you, too, Bunny!" I said through tears of laughter.

"Darlings, stop all of that giggling and do what you were doing before?"

I shot Bunny, the creeper, a you'vegottobefuckingkiddingme look.

"Please, darling?" She pouted and rocked herself back and forth a bit when another set of footsteps approached.

"You did take my camera! That's like taking another woman's bra!" Aunt Janice yanked the camera from her sister's hands and looked at us.

"Hey! Good morning, you two! It's a white Christmas!"

Mom and Janice talked over one another, and Opal whispered, "Now, we need your father to complete the set."

"Bunny. We'd like to get out of bed now. Do you mind?" I pointed at the door.

"Just one photo, darling?"

"I have to admit, you two have a Life magazine quality. It could make for some wonderful photos." Aunt Janice said, framing us with her fingers and thumbs.

"You can't put them on the internet."

"Of course, not!" Bunny said. "

Hey, I'm not really comfortable with-" Opal said, darting her eyes between Bunny and me.

"Please, Roxanne? For the family scrapbook?" Bunny began to pout again.

"What kind of scrapbook are you making, Bunny?!" I shouted.

"One to show your children when you're old like me! Now, look cozy!" Opal sighed and nodded. Bunny squealed with delight, "Just pretend to be sleeping. Janice, how do I turn this on again?"

They chatted over one another for a moment. Opal propped herself up on her elbow and leaned into my ear. "I am very grateful for the shelter in the storm, but I'm not sure I'm this grateful."

CHARLOTTE

*A*fter a 15 minute tutorial on Aunt Janice's camera, Bunny gave up on her button-pushing desires and volunteered Aunt Janice to shoot. We sat up in bed, never letting the covers reveal Opal's black jeans.

After a tornado of entrances and exits, Bunny brought in props! A coffee mug, funny hats, mittens. We posed for shot after Norman Rockwellian shot.

"Okay," I said in a polite but firm tone, "We'd like to get dressed for the day now."

"Oh, just come in your pajamas, darling. We all are."

"You're in heels."

"Footwear optional." They spun out of the room and gently closed the door behind them, leaving soft echoes of "sweet" and "adorable" in their wake.

"Do you have any sweats in that gym bag?"

"Not clean ones."

"You're what, 5 6'?"

"I'm 5 9'. Why?"

"I'm 5 2' which means all of my yoga pants are too long for me." She sprung out of bed and tossed a giant suitcase onto the foot of the bed. After throwing out a lot of pale pink spandex...

"Ah-ha!" she held the leggings above her head triumphantly.

"Welcome to your new pajama pants. Now, gimme your jeans." She tossed the leggings at my head. She propped a fist on her hip, looking like a young Bunny, and made a "gimme" motion with her finger.

"Hi," I pulled the blankets up higher to have the illusion of privacy and started to unbutton my jeans, "I'm Opal Blakewood." I tugged on my zipper, "I'm 32-years old, which means I'm too old to hide from someone's parents." I wiggled the jeans down with one hand while keeping the blanket pulled tightly to my chest. "I spent my childhood years in

45

Japan with my mother and father. I went to college at MIT much to their chagrin. I lived in Arizona for a few years before moving here, I'm divorced, I take my coffee black, and I think llamas are adorable." I tossed my jeans at her.

"Feel better now?!" "No, but now it makes more sense that you've seen me without my shirt on, cuddled with me in bed, and asked for my pants."

OPAL

"*I*'m a nice person. At least, I thought I was a nice person. My ex-wife might disagree. It's been two years, so maybe all of the good memories of the beginning are all that's left.   Coming in for a 20-minute deception to help save a beautiful girl's holiday seemed like an easy win. Would I have done it if she hadn't smelled of vanilla and looked so enticing? Well,…"

Knock, knock, knock. "Are you talking to yourself in there?"

"This is a private conversation, ma'am." She giggled and leaned against the door.

"I wanted to apologize for being so bossy and assuming that you were even still willing to participate in this …"

"Misrepresentation?" I said with toothpaste in my mouth.

"Yeah." I rinsed and opened the door a crack. "It's okay. It will make for a good story."

"Are you a writer?"

"No. But I might become one." We exchanged reassuring smiles with one another.

CHARLOTTE

"So, are you ready for breakfast?"

"Oh, I'm never coming out of this bathroom. It's my home now." She shut the door.

"Wait. What?"

"I know most people wear yoga pants all of the time, but I only wear them at the gym. I feel a little naked. I don't think I should go downstairs like this."

"They are squat proof! And, they're a size too big for me, so they should be perfect for you!" She slowly opened the door, and I saw every muscle striation in her calves and thighs through the leggings. Her silk camisole bellowed where a little belly fat would be on a normal person. Did her shoulders look like that when she was spooning me?

"See what I mean? It's a little revealing for breakfast, don't you think?"

"Nonsense. You look great. And, your arms are the only thing not covered. You're practically dressed like a nun. Off we go!" The words came out faster and faster as my cheeks got redder and redder.

"Breathe." She put her hands on my arms and locked eyes with me.

"I was mostly joking. I can throw my button down over this, and it will be fine." I stepped away and sat on the edge of my bed. I tried to hold it all in, but I couldn't. Tears welled up in my eyes, my body shook, and I started sobbing.

"I'm sorry."

"We've really got to work on this apologizing thing." She said as she took a seat beside me and laced her fingers together between her knees.

"I am, um, feeling a little anxious." I wiped at the tears on my cheeks.

"You don't say."

"Don't make fun."

"I'm not making fun." She unlaced her fingers and wrapped an arm around my shoulder, and began to rock me side to side. "I would never make fun of that."

"It's just so hard to do everything right all of the time. I want to do everything right all of the time."

"Why is that?" She hummed, placing her cheek against my head.

"I don't want to disappoint anyone any more than I have." I felt like hurling.

"How do you think you've disappointed people?"

"I'm not married. Bunny thinks I should be married."

"Is that what you think?"

"No. 'Married' comes after 'fall in love', you know?"

"Right. What else?"

"I don't know. I just don't feel good enough lately. Especially with Rex leaving…"

"Who's opinion is the most important?" She pulled away and brought her curled finger to my chin. "Who's opinion is the most important to you?"

"I don't know. Bunny's?"

"No. Yours. You have to hit your own standards and no one else's. The sooner you realize that all of this other stuff will just melt away." She held my gaze there for what felt like an eternity. I could feel myself leaning closer to her.

"French toast or pancakes!" And, the bedroom door flew open for the second time that morning.

CHARLOTTE

Opal dug out a wrinkled flannel shirt from her gym bag, and we walked down the stairs. The smell of French toast filled the air. My dad was at the griddle wearing his "Kiss The Cook" apron, which featured an hourglass-figured woman's torso in a pink bikini.

"Classy, dad." I leaned in and kissed him on the cheek. He smiled, nodded, and went back to flipping French toast.

Aunt Janice and Bunny were exchanging a knowing glance over coffee mugs.

"Why are the two of you looking at each other like that?" I reached over and dipped a strawberry into a bowl of freshly whipped cream.

"Your mother said she walked in on you…" Aunt Janice said, waggling her eyebrows. Mom held her hands up in defense.

"I just said…"

"She didn't see anything." I said flatly, grabbing a handful of strawberries this time. But she did see something. Opal barely even knew my name, but she took the time to comfort me and calm me down.

"I clearly was interrupting a private moment, and for that, I do apologize. I'll remember to knock in the future."

"Thank you, Bunny."

"You're welcome, dear heart." she squeezed my chin between her thumb and finger.

My mother may be chatty, dramatic, and high maintenance, and she may have standards that are impossible to meet, but she does love me.

Breakfast was pretty mellow after that. We drank our coffee and stuffed ourselves with French toast, strawberries, fresh whipped cream, and then more coffee. Opal held her own with Aunt Janice.

Turns out, swapping travel stories is where Opal lives! She actually did hike that glacier. She's been everywhere! She and Aunt Janice talked about glaciers, mountain climbing, climate change, and somehow they ended up on the topic of adventure vacationing. I'm pretty sure they made plans for the summer.

"She's marvelous, darling." Bunny leaned against the kitchen island and gesture to Opal, who was going on about Patagonia in the breakfast nook with Aunt Janice. Dad was leaning against the entry frame, smiling and sipping coffee from his World's Greatest Grandma mug. "She is beautiful, well-traveled, highly educated. Most importantly," she held my hands," she seems to make you very happy." Bunny leaned in and squeezed my shoulders, kissing my forehead.

She had always wanted a big family. After she had me, she had cervical cancer. She had to have a hysterectomy. She's been cancer-free ever since. But, she always wanted a bigger family.

It was no secret that she was counting on me to give her a few grandchildren. Being a lesbian put a damper on her original dream. Then, she started reading articles about how same-sex couples were growing their families.

Her dream expanded from one or two grandchildren to, and I quote, "Darling, you can have five, six, or maybe even seven children without a single stretch mark if you plan accordingly!"

"I am elated for you." She walked towards the breakfast nook and joined everyone.

Looking on as a casual observer, you'd think Opal had been one of the family for years. It was all so surreal. I tried to imagine what it would be like if Roxanne were in her place.

Roxanne is a bit more old-school jock. I would have never said this when we were together, but she definitely peaked in high school.

I was jarred out of my own thoughts when I heard Bunny say, "And this is her in the 5th-grade talent show doing a piece from Hamlet..."

"Mother! Drop your weapon! Now, step away from the photo album!"

CHARLOTTE

Ding. Roxanne Breedlove posted a photo on LookPage.
          I knew not to click it as I was clicking it. There in plain view of god and everybody was a picture of Rex and that curly-haired bitch from accounting snuggling in front of a Christmas tree.

Caption: Such a fun night with my girl celebrating our first Christmas.

"I shouldn't read the comments. No. That would be unnecessary," I mumbled to myself as I swiped up and saw the heart and kissy-face emojis sent by family members I had never met and coworker that I suddenly realized a) knew about this for a while, and b) didn't tell me. I could feel my face becoming hot. The polite chatter in the background suddenly became too much to handle.

"We're going out for a bit!"

OPAL

"*Y*ou aren't driving in this, surely," Bunny said, playing with her pearls nervously.

"No, we're going to walk the property. I want to show her around a bit."

She wrapped a gray knit scarf around her neck. I took her coat from the coat closet and held it open for her. She spun into it. A faint hint of vanilla floated passed me.

Bunny blustered about us, tucking our scarves around our necks and promising hot chocolate upon our return. She was a force of nature, but it is all good nature like a TV mom from a black and white show.

From the front of the house in the dark, the Greene's home looked like your typical upscale home. I knew they had a large piece of land, because their closest neighbors were about two miles on either side.

When we stepped out on the back porch and into the cold, I saw an open backyard that bumped up against Tennessee woods.

"Is that wooded area there yours as well?"

"Yep. I grew up in those woods."

"That explains a lot." She backhanded me in the stomach.

"Come on. I'll show you around." I walked through the snow in borrowed muck boots following close behind Charlotte.

"So, this is it." She spread her arms as if to take it all in. "See that barn over there? That's ours too. It used to be a working barn. Horses, sheep, chickens…"

"Not anymore?"

"Nope."

"Why not?"

"Bunny said it was too much work for the two of them. She said she'd be happy to get animals again if I move back home or if I…"

She laughed and shook her head.

"If you what?"

"Nothing. It doesn't matter." She walked a few steps in front of me, putting distance between her and the conversation. I took a few quick steps to catch up.

"So, what's in the barn now."

"Let me show you."

The barn was further away than it looked. It sat atop a small hill. A giant wreath hung on the side. There was a two-tier deck on the side of the barn with built-in benches. A staircase led from the patio up to the upper floor deck, where there were two french doors that led inside the loft area of the barn.

We started up the stairs taking care to not slip on the snow and layer of ice beneath it. When we reached the top, she pulled at an iron statue of a hen that had frozen to the small wooden table outside the door. It wouldn't budge. She tried both hands, but nothing.

"Damn it. Well, the tour ends here. The key is under that thing, and it's practically welded on there."

"May I?" I pointed to the hen with my gloved hands.

"You can try, but I don't think…"

I removed my gloves and gave the statue a good tug. It broke away instantly. I looked at the bottom and turned the latch beneath and revealed a small key. I dumped the key into her mittened paw. Charlotte looked at me, looked at the key, and back at me.

"I have to say it." She said matter-of-factly.

"I know you do."

"I'm gonna say it."

"I wouldn't expect you not to say it." A Cheshire grin swept across her face.

"I loosened it."

CHARLOTTE

*I*t all started with a single gift. Bunny and I got dad a pool table for Father's Day. Then, she got him a jukebox for Valentine's Day with all of their favorite songs programmed in it. Then, the recliner came from Aunt Janice, a pinball machine from the Napiers, and so on and so on. Before we even knew what we had done, the Dad Loft had been born.

"Let me turn the heat up, and then I'll give you a tour." I jogged to the gas fireplace and clicked it on. When I turned to look at Opal, she was smiling and looking around, taking in all of the little nicknacks on the walls and mismatched pieces of furniture.

"So this is my dad's thinking place. All of the photographs are Aunt Janice's work, of course. The jukebox works. Over here," I stepped into the room a little further, "is the bathroom, and this is an office slash library. And, here," I said, pushing through the saloon doors, "is the kitchenette."

She took her hands out of her pockets and started removing her gloves.

"What do you think?" I asked. "This is great. I feel like I understand your dad a little more now."

She walked back toward the French doors dropping her coat, gloves, and scarf on the brown leather sofa. She slid her hand over the mother of pearl inlay on the pool table.

"Do you play?" I asked.

"I did when I was in college." I removed my winter gear and reached inside the mini-fridge for a couple of dark beers. I popped the caps and offered one to Opal.

"Up for a game?"

CHARLOTTE

"*E*ight ball. Corner pocket." The balls clanked together, and I was O for two.

"Played a little in college, my ass." She laughed and hung her head.

"I swear. I haven't played since I was...how old are you again?"

"Twenty-six"."

"Yeah, I haven't played since I was your age."

"Like you're so old, granny!"

"Six years is a lot. Your whole life can change in six years." She moved around the table, gathering the balls in the wrack.

"Here's hoping!" I raised my beer.

"Is your life so bad. I mean besides the mattress thing." I sat my beer down and pulled my phone from my back pocket.

After a few strategic swipes, I tossed the phone on the table in front of her.

"Which one is her?"

"The butch one."

Opal held the phone close to her face and pulled it away

again. She set the phone down, and shoved one hand in her pocket and scratched her head with the other.

"Eh. You can do better."

"You don't even know me." I ran my thumb over the mouth of the empty bottle. "I work with both of them."

Opal leaned against the table.

"The other girl, the girly one. Her name is Rachel. Rachel is Roxanne's "secret agent" in accounting." I scooted over on the couch and snatched Opal's half-full beer bottle from the edge of the side table.

She sighed and puffed her cheeks out.

"She's supposed to be here right now." Tears welled up, and my cheeks were warm. "Last week, everything was normal. We went to the grocery store, watched Law & Order reruns, and made plans for her to meet my parents finally. I mean…How long has she been seeing her?!"

Opal pushed the Field & Stream magazines on the coffee table to the side and sat across from me. She rested her elbows on her knees and pressed woven fingers to her lips.

"You look like you want to say something."

"I do." She took her beer out of my hands and took a long swig. "My ex-wife ran out on me while I was at work. My company had just gone public, and I was under a lot of pressure to perform."

"Company? You're a Tag-A-Ride driver?"

"I am the first Tag-A-Ride driver."

OPAL

*H*er eyebrows knitted together in front, and she pulled her legs up into her chest. "Explain more, please."

"When I was in college, I needed to earn money. The only asset I had was a car that my parents gave me. I wanted to pay them back for it, but I couldn't work a job with regular shifts taking the course load I was taking. So, I started giving people rides for extra money.

Most people didn't carry cash on them, so they'd owe me. I wanted to make it easier for my friends to pay me back for the rides, so I made an app. Before I knew it, I had a business. You follow me? You look confused?"

"A little. I mean," she closed her eyes and waved her hands to clear the previous statement from the air, "I understand the whole you made an app part. I don't understand the part where you picked me up at the airport as a driver."

"My therapist thought…"

Charlotte's body slumped into the couch a little further, recoiling away from me.

"I'm not violent or anything. It's okay."

She nodded.

"There was a lot of pressure on me after my business went public, and my wife left me, right? So, I had regular panic attacks. A lot like the one you were having this morning. Nothing dangerous, but crippling at times. They were keeping me from working and taking care of myself generally.

I went to see someone, the therapist, and she thought I should take a break from people that makes demands on me. I did, and I got better. I haven't had a panic attack in a long time.

I wanted to go back to work, but she thought it would be best to ease into it. Put myself in situations where people are putting only a little pressure on me to perform. So, I started driving again."

She stared at me.

"You were my first ride…"

The edges of her mouth turned down. Her shoulders began to tremble, and then the sobbing started.

"No. No, no, no." I moved beside her on the couch and wrapped my arm around her shoulders.

"I cannot believe this! You are literally trying to reenter the world, and I've basically kidnapped you and have done nothing but ask you for stuff since we met! Take me to my mom's house! Take a picture with! Smile while you're at it. I made you sleep on the floor! You're going to be in therapy for the rest of your life because of me!"

I couldn't help it. I laughed. I laughed hard.

"You are so your mother's daughter, you know that?"

"Oh, god!" She sobbed with her head in her hands.

"Hey. Hey." I whispered softly to her and adjusted myself on the couch so she could lean into me. "It's a compliment."

I held her there with her head pressed against my heart in silence for a moment.

"I'm better for it all," I said, running her fingers through the ends of her hair. "I'm better for my ex-wife leaving because we weren't happy. Not really. When I thought we were happy, I wasn't wrong, but it wasn't the kind of happy I want for myself. You'll get over this. She wasn't worth your time anymore. She took your fucking mattress."

We both laughed at that one.

"Is there anything I can do to make you happy at this moment right now?"

"Yes."

My heart became a drum. Then, she said, "Will you let me finish your beer?"

CHARLOTTE

"*L*et's play one more game before we head back. I don't want to look like I've been crying when we get back to the house."

She handed me her bottle and started racking the balls.

"Music?" I asked.

"Sure." I selected Bernadette by the Four Tops. I saw Opal smile out of the corner of my eye.

"Like this one?"

"Yeah." We had just unburdened ourselves to one another, and now, we were speaking in short sentences.

"Hey, I'm-"

"Breaking this time?" She smiled as she cut me off from saying it. We were silent through the game until I called

"Eight ball. Far corner." I struck the cue ball hard, and it made a sharp spin into the center pocket.

"Do over." She took the ball from the pocket and placed it back where it was.

"No," I said, "A scratched on the eight ball. I lose. You win, my friend."

"You almost had it. Try again." I sighed, chalked my stick, and took the shot again. Same results.

"I think the beers have killed my shot-making abilities."

"I don't buy it. One more time."

"Opal, I can't make the shot. Take your victory like a champ." I pumped my fist in the air. "All, hail! Opal, the destroyer!"

She walked around me and sat the ball back. She swept her arm out to the side as if to say your shot is ready, ma'am.

"One more time." I leaned over the table and crooked my finger around the stick.

"There's your problem." She leaned beside me.

"Aim a little to the right and a little higher."

"Like this?" "Almost. Here." She placed her hand on the small of my back and leaned forward, wrapping her left hand around mine. I felt her hip brush against mine. Without my permission, my heart pounded a little harder, and my cheeks got warmer. I turned to look at her, and when I did, it happened...

OPAL

$\mathcal{W}$e kissed.

We must have turned our heads at the same time. I turned my head quickly and stepped away from the table.

"I didn't mean to do that," Charlotte said.

"No, I didn't either." I shoved my hands into my pockets like if I did it well enough, I might just disappear into my pockets.

"Are we cool?"

"Yep."

"We should head back then?"

"Yeah, I think so."

We walked back to the house in silence and with at least four feet between us at all times. My hands were blocks of ice in my coat pocket, but I wasn't about to ask for an escort back to get my gloves.

"You can leave the mucks out on the mat inside the door." She said, kicking off her muck boots and heading upstairs.

"Should I -"

"I think you should stay down here for a second."

Her words cut mine off as she ran upstairs. I heard the slam of her bedroom door and the faint sounds of a lock. The house was intensely quiet, aside from a murmuring coming from the living area. I had no idea what to do with myself, so I headed toward the sound.

Lewis was in his chair with his feet on a matching ottoman watching curling. His eyes were half-open. In one hand, he had the remote, and in the other hand, he was flipping a quarter over his knuckles.

I rounded the loveseat and sat on the end, hugging a pillow to my chest. The curly blonde ringlets atop Lewis's head didn't move a bit as he turned to me, nodded, and went back to watching the game.

"Bunny and Janice are napping." He said.

"Sounds nice."

"It is." He closed his eyes all the way, and a small snore escaped him.

CHARLOTTE

"*H*ey, this is fine. This is no big deal. You're single. You're allowed to kiss people who are practically strangers."

My reflection scolded and reassured me.

"Also, Opal is hot, so ... That doesn't matter! It was an accident. You weren't taking advantage of her!

Now, be a big girl, and tell her that. Also, tell her you liked it.

No! Don't do that last part. Do the first part. We. Have. A. Plan."

I high-fived myself in the mirror and unlocked my door.

Bunny and Aunt Janice were either sleeping or up to no good planning something in a quiet corner of the house because all I could hear was dad snoring. When I saw no sign of Opal in the kitchen or den, I looked out the window and saw her SUV still in the driveway with snow up to the tops of the tires.

I headed toward the living room and saw the top of dad's head poking above the back of his chair. The gentle hum of sleep filled the room and blended in nicely with the curling commentary. That's when I saw Opal staring at the television and squeezing a pillow.

"Hey," I whispered, "Can we talk?"

She nodded.

I motion for her to follow me upstairs, and she complied. I softly shut and locked the door behind me. Opal was looking out the window at the mounds of snow along the side of the road.

"Looks like they're clearing the roads. I should be able to get out of here tomorrow if there isn't another wave of snow."

"Or you could stay?" The words just came out.

She looked over her shoulder at me. I picked at my thumbnail as she walked toward me. She was about to say something when I held up my hands to stop her.

"Before you say anything, I want to apologize. For real. Not just because it's a habit."

I gestured for her to sit on the bed in front of me.

"I was not meaning to take advantage of you up there. We must have turned our heads at the same time, or -"

"You thought you took advantage of me?" The corner of Opal's mouth turned up.

"Well, yeah. You had just told me all of that stuff. You were vulnerable. I thought, maybe I…"

"We did just happen to turn our heads at the same time. I was afraid you thought I was taking advantage of you." She chuckled to herself, mostly. She rubbed her hands over her face. "Geez."

Her hands fell to her knees with a slap. I sat beside her on the bed and fell backward, covering my face with a pillow.

"Could you do me a favor and just press down on this pillow for me? I'd like to be put out of my misery for good, please." My words muffled against the pillow.

"Then, who would smother me?" She said, falling back and landing beside me. She reached over and took the pillow tossing it to the head of the bed.

"Do you believe in fate?" I asked between chuckles.

"I didn't."

CHARLOTTE

*I*t was one of those awakenings that you fight against. I was so warm and comfortable. I kept telling myself not to open my eyes. I could easily go right back to sleep. I closed my eyes tighter, but in the distance, I heard music and chatter.

I blinked my eyes open and felt a strong arm wrapped around me. I reached back and grabbed Opal's leg. She jolted behind me and took a sharp inhale.

"Hey," she spoke softly, "when did we…?"

"I have no idea. We must have passed out around the same time." She slid her arm out and untangled herself from me.

"Turning our heads at the same time. Falling asleep at the same time. I think this makes us friends now."

"I think so. We know so much about each other." I slathered on the sarcasm.

"We really do, Charlotte Greene with an E who's favorite color is pink and takes little coffee with her cream."

"I suppose you're right, Ms. Opal Blakewood who was the first Tag-A-Ride driver, takes her coffee black, grew up in

Japan, and who's favorite color is…What is your favorite color?"

"You can't tell?"

"Black!" I said enthusiastically.

"Nope." She laughed.

"You'll never guess it in a million years."

"Mustard?"

"Nope." She stood and stretched.

"Green of any kind?"

"I'll give you a hint. May I?" She held up her hands, and when I nodded, she ran her thumb over my lips. She held her thumb in front of me. A light smudge of my pale lipstick shown on it.

"Pink?"

She blushed.

"Powder pink?" I asked again.

She stuffed her hands in her pockets, sucked in her lips, and nodded.

"But, you are so…"

"Dark? Gothic? Emo, I think is a thing too?"

"Yeah."

"I like to wear black and grey, because I don't want to have to think about what I'm wearing. I'm kind of a minimalist." She tugged at the hem of my baby pink sweater. Her finger grazed my stomach, "But I've always loved to look at pale pinks."

I cleared my throat. "About before…in the loft of the barn…"

Knock, knock, knock!

Our heads spun around to face the door.

"Darlings," Bunny shouted through the door, "It's time to wake up! It's party time! Get your sweaters on, and come downstairs! Aunt Janice set up a photo booth, and dad made a cheese log!"

"We'll be right down, Mrs. Greene."

"Call me, Bunny, darling! You're family!" She sang as she clicked away.

"You were saying," she said.

"Oh, it's not important," I turned toward the door, but her hand caught my cheek, cradling it and turning my eyes to meet hers.

Her other hand moved from the hem of my sweater to the small of my back. She curled her finger beneath my chin and brought my lips up to meet hers.

OPAL

My body wanted to take over, but my brain was doing an excellent job of keeping me at bay.

One kiss, I thought to myself, but I knew one wouldn't be enough.

The feeling of her body pressed against me was the most relaxing feeling I had ever experienced. It felt like…home.

Her hand reached up to mine. She released me from the kiss and stared into my eyes. I thought she was breaking away from the moment, but she didn't. She guided my hand from her chin down to meet my other.

I wove my fingers together behind her back and drew her in close to me. She gripped my shirt and stood on her tiptoes to kiss me again, and again, and, thank god, again.

She pulled at my shirt hard, causing me to fall on top of her on the bed. I swept her hair to one side and kissed the delicate curve of her neck.

"You smell like heaven."

"Vanilla oil," she breathed.

"I knew it," I said into her jawline.

We wove the fingers of one hand together while my other

hand slid beneath her to the small of her back and pulled us closer together. Our breath became become rapid and rhythmic when…

Knock, knock, knock. "Darlings! Have you fallen asleep again?" Bunny shouted through the door.

OPAL

It had been a long time since I had looked at anyone romantically, and here I was kissing Charlotte.

Charlotte.

My whole body was humming after that...whatever that was.

We straighten ourselves out enough to walk downstairs. We didn't bother to put on the ugly sweaters. Charlotte held my hand and led me down the staircase.

When we hit the bottom floor, we were surrounded by the buzzing of a proper Ugly Sweater Christmas party.

"How did she do all of this?" I asked. Charlotte stood with her mouth open and shaking her head.

"Everybody," Aunt Janice shouted as she attached herself to the end of a conga line that was dancing from the living room to the kitchen, "Richard spiked the egg nog twice!"

"Aunt Janice," Charlotte tugged at a piece of glittering garland dangling from Aunt Janice's hair, "How did all of these people get here."

"Girls! I'm so glad our party planning didn't wake you,

but judging from those hairdos, sleep wasn't the only thing you were getting!" She snorted and laughed.

"Aunt Janice..."

"Well, the Napiers LookPage-ed us after Bunny posted the party was canceled because of the snow. And, they said they were willing to ride their horses over." Aunt Janice swayed and held the railing with both hands.

"These people are not he Napiers. I don't even see the Napiers here."

"They hitched up a sleigh and picked up everyone in the area. Then, Marcy and that other woman rode their horses over and dragged some folks in a sledge behind them."

"You mean sleigh?"

"Yes! A sleigh! They have Clydesdales, the Napiers, and an eight-person sleigh. So, they went around the neighborhood twice. We put the horses up in the barn. Thank you for turning the heat on up there. Good thinking," she swayed a bit as Lewis spun passed with a plate of pigs in a blanket, "So the horses are fine. The people are fine. We're having a party!"

"Janice," I said, reaching for her arm, "Janice, when you see Bunny can you tell her we're mingling. There are so many people here, I'm afraid we might miss her."

"No problem, travel buddy." She slapped my cheek with each word.

"Walter! You're alive!" We watched her dance-off. Charlotte looked at me inquisitively. I wrapped her arm in mine and led her back to her room to pick up right where we left off.

CHARLOTTE

*S*unlight streamed through the sheer curtains. I could feel Opal's breath against the back of my neck. Flashes from only hours ago rushed over me.

Me locking the door. Her grabbing handfuls of my hair as she kissed me like she was starving. Me finding skin beneath black silk.

"Mmm." She hummed into my hair, pulling me away from the replay. I rolled over and propped myself up on my elbow.

"Good morning."

"Good morning to you too."

"So…"

"Again?" she said, grinning deviously.

"Anytime you're ready." She grabbed hold of me and pull me on top of her. She wrapped her arms around my waist, securing me in place.

"What time is it?"

"It doesn't matter," I said, stealing kisses from her swollen lips, "We're snowed in, remember? School's out. It's a snow day."

"Well, in that case," We rolled, and she crashed into me like a wave taking my face in her hands.

Knock. Knock. Knock.

"Darlings!" Bunny sang into the door. Opal sighed hard and dropped her head into the crook of my neck.

"Morning, Bunny," I said, "We're not all the way awake yet."

"Well, hurry up, dear. It's Tree Day after all."

"Ah, yes. Of course," I muttered.

"Tree Day? Decorating?" Opal asked quietly.

"Chopping and decorating, darling!" Bunny said into the solid mahogany.

"Want to go tree hunting?"

CHARLOTTE

*B*rushing your teeth together is the height of intimacy.

I kept wondering how did I ended up here brushing my teeth beside my Tag-A-Ride driver who was actually the creator and owner of Tag-A-Ride, meaning she was smart, successful, and so, so, so sexy?

I was so relaxed with her. My hair even felt calmer. Her fingers in my hair…"Mmm…"

She nudged my hips and brought me out of my daydream. "You still with me?"

I had apparently been brushing the same side for a while. She walked behind me and wrapped her arms around me, resting her chin on my shoulder.

"Yeah. I was just thinking."

"Want to tell me about it?"

"I'd rather show you," I spun and kissed her full on the lips and took a few steps back, "But, alas, dear heart, I cannot. It is tree day."

Tree Day tradition started when my dad was a child. On Christmas eve, he and his siblings would head out behind

81

their house and chop down the most beautiful Christmas tree they could find.

My dad and I kept the tradition alive by going out back and hunting for a tree every Christmas eve ourselves while Bunny stayed home to made hot chocolate and crepes for our return. We'd spend the afternoon decorating the tree together.

I felt a hand on the small of my back and then a gentle kiss on my cheek. "Good morning again."

My cheeks bloomed with flush, "Good morning again." I took a look at her as she rounded me and sat on the barstool beside me. She was wearing her black jeans and silk button-down."

"Do you want to do some laundry later?"

"If I'm staying, that would be great."

"Oh, I don't think you're ever leaving." I stood and wrapped my arms around her neck.

"Is that a fact, ma'am?"

"It is."

"Good morning, my angels! It's tree day!" Bunny spiraled through the room kissing our cheeks before landing behind the island.

"Let's talk strategy."

"Not too wide. Not too tall." I said.

"Just right!" She squealed.

"No Charlie Brown trees."

"No Charlie Brown trees." She confirmed.

"Where are we going to purchase this non-Charlie Brown tree, honey?"

She called me honey. Butterflies do not begin to describe the sensation in my stomach. If I had been near a fainting couch, I would have used it. Nothing quite compares to the adoration of the person you adore.

"We ain't going to no tree lot, ma'am. This is Tennessee."

OPAL

*I*t was straight out of classic American literature. We donned hats with earflaps, muck boots, and plaid shirts. Charlotte slung an ax over her shoulder and reached a hand out for me.

"I don't know if I want to be attached to you while you're carrying that thing."

"I promise not to chop you up and leave in the woods." She wrapped a mittened hand around mine, "I'll feed you to the Napier's pigs."

"Good. I don't want all this muscle I spent years building going to waste. What was it all for if not a delightful Christmas dinner for some piggies?"

"We're dark."

"Yeah, but it works, doesn't it?" Lewis held a handsaw overhead and quietly declared, "Charge." We marched through the wet snow toward the tree line.

A few slips and tumbles later, we were standing in a small patch of cypress trees. A couple of small stumps were scattered about, and saplings were poking through the snow.

"Okay," Charlotte clapped her mittens, "Rules."

"There are rules?"

"Yes. One, we don't take homes. We look before we chop."

"Okay."

"Okay." There was a brief pause. Bird song from some-where. The quiet steps of Lewis.

"You said rules."

"I can't think of a second rule right now." I caught her shoulder before she spun away and pulled her in close.

"You're adorable. Do you know that?" Her warm lips crashed into mine, and then my body crashed into a small tree behind me.

Snow tumbled from the branches coating us in winter.

"Cold. Cold. Cold." She said, jumping and flailing about. A mound of snow sat unmoved on top of her hat.

"Hold still," I said as I mussed my hair and shook the lapels of my jacket. I fashioned a small ball of snow in my hands and sat on top of the mound on her hat.

"Are you…"

"Making a tiny snowman on your head?"

"Yes?"

"Yes."

CHARLOTTE

I reached into my coat pocket and handed Opal my phone.

"I want to see this."

"He's not done yet. One sec," she reached behind her and broke a little twig into tinier pieces,

"Arms and nose. Okay. He's finished."

I made some 'what's on my head' faces for a few pictures.

"Come here for a sec." I waved her over, "Take a picture with me."

She put her arm around me, leaned in, and opened her mouth wide.

"Are you eating my snowman?!" She snapped away as she pretended to eat the little snowman. I carefully removed my hat and placed it on her, snowman and all. I had to hold it in place, but it was pretty cute.

"I found him!" Lewis's quiet voice trickled through tree limbs.

"Him?" she asked.

"The tree."

OPAL

Since Charlotte and Lewis handled the choosing and chopping of the tree, I volunteered to drag it back to the house.

I held a small tree limb with my hand, and Charlotte wrapped her arm in my mine, warming my free hand in hers.

"Tree Day!" shouted Aunt Janice as she hefted her camera over her shoulder.

"Tree Day!" Lewis and Charlotte shouted.

Janice and Bunny had placed a large, metal Christmas tree stand in the corner of the living room. Lewis and I positioned it on the stand and turned the tree around in circles until Bunny found the perfect side.

"It's just marvelous, darlings! Now, come," she wrapped her arm in mine, "let me make you all some hot chocolate, and perhaps, you could help me bring the decorations into the living room, darling?" She asked, patting my forearm.

"Of course, Mrs. Greene."

"Bunny, dear. Call me 'Bunny' or 'mom.' Either way," she flitted her fingers through the air.

"Oh, she can call you 'mom,' but I can't."

"I don't make the rules, dear, I just honor them."

"You do make the rules!"

"I suppose I do. All hail, Queen Bunny!"

OPAL

$\mathcal{T}$he sunset early as it does in winter, and we were all in our pajamas once again. My clothes smelled of fabric softener. It was nice to have my own clothes back on.

"Charades, darlings! Gather! Gather! Bring wine and cheese, Janice!" I sat in the corner, watching the Greene family buzz about and sipping a cup of hot, green tea.

Bunny clicked back and forth between the coffee table and roll top desk. She was writing feverishly on sheets of paper, folding them, and dropping them in a mirrored bowl. Lewis was sitting in his overstuffed chair, which he had turned to watch Bunny in her frenzy. Janice loaded her arms with wine. Charlotte was ladling soup into a glass container for tomorrow.

It was all so surreal. Like being in one of those cozy Christmas movies that I had watched my whole life and made fun of. But it was nice. Warm fire, warm drinks, warm food. The smell of fresh pine filling the room. I was inside a Christmas card.

"What?" Charlotte smiled.

"Huh? Me? Nothing."

"You were staring."

"I was just thinking," I lifted the hot mug to my lips, "soup for breakfast sounds pretty good."

"It does, doesn't it. Let's do that tomorrow." She slapped a red lid onto the container and pushed down the corner.

"Unless, I mean, if you need to go…"

I stood and joined her at the counter, "How about tomorrow we go back to my place?"

She arched a suspicious eyebrow at me.

"No, no," I chuckled, "I mean so you can see where I live. Maybe, I can cook lunch for you." I took her hand in mine and kissed it softly.

"You always do that."

"Do what?"

"Whenever you kiss me, you go 'mmm.' Why is that?"

"I didn't even notice I was doing it. Mmm…," I hummed, kissing her hand again.

"I heard it that time. Do you always smell like this?"

"Like what?"

"The vanilla and cookie smell."

"Yeah, I guess."

"Heavenly." I sighed.

"Lunch at your place sounds great." She put two warm hands on my cheeks and stood on her tiptoes to kiss me.

"Charlotte! Grab the crackers and cheese tray in the fridge, please. Aunt Janice is too tipsy to stand up. Thank you, darling." Bunny sang from the living room.

We broke away from one another, and I grabbed the tray while she put the soup in the fridge. It was so domestic.

CHARLOTTE

"*M*onkey pants!" Aunt Janice chortled.

"Monkey pants? Really, darling? I know it's vacation, but I'm about to cut you off!" Bunny said, placing a firm fist on her hip.

"I'm sorry. I'm sorry." Aunt Janice wiped the tears from her eyes.

"Let's start again. Lewis, can we start again." He gently nodded and grinned. Bunny held up four fingers.

"Four words." Shouted Aunt Janice.

Bunny held up one finger.

"First word."

Knock, knock.

Frustration spread across Bunny's face.

"You all carry on. I'll get it." Opal said before she turned to kiss the top of my head.

"Thank you, darling." She smiled sweetly and turned to Aunt Janice.

"Focus."

Indistinct murmuring from the foyer caused me to lean back on the sofa to see if I could get a glimpse of which neighbor had come to visit. Opal peered at me from over her shoulder. She held up a finger to the visitor and walked to the entryway in socked feet.

"Um…Charlotte. Could you come here for a moment?" She looked pale. Paler than usual.

"Monkey!" Shouted Aunt Janice

"Time," Lewis whispered with a smile.

"Planet of the Apes, Janice. Planet. Of. The. Apes!"

"I thought you said it was a book."

"It is a book?"

"It was a book first, darling."

"Wasn't called Monkey Planet when it was first released?"

They continued talking over one another, and I slide out of the line of fire to join Opal. My smile quickly faded when I saw who was at the door.

"Roxanne?"

OPAL

"Hey, Char."

The two of them held a silent stare. Bunny and Janice were giggling and insulting each other.

"What the hell are you doing here?"

"I came to talk." She fumbled a small box in her hands. "And, to bring your Christmas present."

Jewelry. It was definitely jewelry.

"I'll give you two a moment."

"No. This isn't going to take long. You can stay."

"Who is this?" Roxanne furrowed her brows and pointed an accusatory finger at me.

"I'm Opal," I extended my hand, "Opal Blakewood."

"Roxanne. Johnston." She shook my hand slowly and held it longer than I particularly like. "How do you two know each other?"

"She was my Tag-A-Ride driver." Charlotte waved her hand in the air as if dismissing me altogether.

"What the hell are you doing here?" She said sternly.

"If you'll excuse me," I said as I turned toward the stairs.

CHARLOTTE

"*U*nless there's a mattress and a handwritten apology in that box, I'm not interested," I whisper shouted at Roxanne as I stepped closer, hoping not to draw any attention.

"I deserve that." She nodded and fumbled the box. "You and I were getting serious, right?"

"Yeah," I said, crossing my arms and letting the no-shit-sherlock attitude drip off my single-word response.

"Well, I got nervous, and I ran away."

"You ran to Rachel."

She sighed, "I ran to Rachel."

"How was your first Christmas with," I made violent air quotes with my fingers, "your girl?"

"We broke up." She hung her head and looked at me with puppy dog eyes.

"That's a record or something. What was it? One? Two days?"

"We broke up because I didn't want to be with her." She took my hands and cupped them together, placing the box in them. "I want to be with you."

I looked at her overly gelled hair, blue scarf, and navy peacoat. I looked at the box that matched her ensemble. Her ensemble and the box that matched her freshly cleaned sneakers. I thought about how coldly she left me. I thought about LookPage posts. I thought about the mattress.

"Charlotte..."Roxanne said as she knelt down on one knee. "Charlotte Greene, will you..."

"Darling, are you leaving?!"

OPAL

I don't know how long I had been standing there staring at this very private moment, but it had been long enough to get the attention of Bunny. And then, Janice. And then, Lewis. Bunny charged toward me with arms outstretched and a worried look on her face.

"Are you okay? Is something the matter, dear? You look positively stricken."

"Oh." I felt my mouth close. "I, um, I need to head out I'm afraid."

Janice tapped rapidly on Bunny's shoulder as she began to interrogate me. "Bunny…" she said, pointing to the now kneeling Roxanne and the statue that was once Charlotte.

"What on Earth?!" Bunny exclaimed.

I gripped my gym bag in my left hand and reached out to shake Lewis's hand. The corners of his lips curled down, and he placed his left hand on my shoulder. His eyes were apologetic and kind. Janice and Bunny moved in a pack toward Charlotte and the real Roxanne.

"What the hell is this?" Janice asked, placing her hands on her hips.

"Yes! What she said!" Bunny shrilled.

Charlotte looked over her shoulder and met the tiny mob's gaze before looking between them to see me release Lewis's hand and head toward her.

"Opal, wait." She gripped my forearm and gave it a squeeze. "Please, wait."

"It's okay, Charlotte." I bent and kissed her cheek. I pressed my cheek against hers and whispered, "Happy Christmas."

Her body relaxed, giving up to gravity. I pressed down on the lever doorknob and made my way through the small mound of snow slush left on the driveway.

CHARLOTTE

"We're waiting." Bunny tapped her foot theatrically.

"I...uh...this is..." I swept my gaze to the kneeling Roxanne, "This is..."

She stood and pocketed the box. "I'm Roxanne Johnston, Mrs. Greene. Charlotte's girlfriend."

"Oh, really?" Bunny asked exasperation on every vowel.

Roxanne looked at Bunny and at me. She looked confused.

"Yes, ma'am." She set her eyes on me. "I thought they were expecting me, Char."

"Char-lotte." Bunny corrected. Roxanne moved her attention to Aunt Janice.

"You must be Janice. It's so nice to meet you finally. Thank you for the lovely prints. We designed our entire bedroom around them, didn't we, Char...?"

Bunny glared a scathing glare at Roxanne.

"Charlotte," Roxanne said, throwing an arm over my shoulder.

"You better come with me." Dad's quiet voice pierced the

awkwardness. He took the frightened and confused animal that was Roxanne by the shoulders and guided her to the kitchen. I heard whispers of sandwiches and lemonade as they walked away. Then, there were three.

Bunny took a deep breath and shook out her hands. Her gold jewelry clinked against each other.

"Who the hell is that?!" Aunt Janice bent over in the whisper scream and pointed with eyes wide toward the kitchen. "Who the hell was in this house with us for the last three days?!"

"Sister, dear. Let's take a breath."

I shuttered and looked at Bunny in shock.

"Take…a…breath?" I asked.

"Yes, darling. Roxanne said, well, the other Roxanne said it helps with processing thoughts and emotions. So, let's all just take a breath." She reached out her hands for us to hold them. Bunny quirked an eyebrow at us and looked at our other hands. We immediately reached out to hold them.

We took two long, deep breaths together. I felt the tension move from my jaw to chest. From my chest to the floor.

Bunny sighed and released our hands. She shrugged. Clapped her hands together. Then, I heard Bunny say, quietly, "Now. Let's talk."

OPAL

I had no idea why I was crying. We had only just met. Charlotte and Roxanne have a history. I barely knew her anyway.

The drive home was slow. I was able to navigate out of Charlotte's neighborhood, but it took some finesse. The ice had melted to puddles during the day, but as the sunset, little patches of ice had developed. Getting back to the highway took half an hour when it should have only taken ten or fifteen minutes. It took an hour total to get me back to the real world. Back to my life. My condo.

I dropped my gym bag on the floor and tossed my wallet, keys, and phone into a wooden dish on the accent table. I cupped hands and blew hot breath into them. My fingers were stiff from the cold.

I took a look around and nodded at my quiet, clean home. I had never noticed the smell of my condo before. Not really. Sandalwood. Faint jasmine. Clean. Nice, but not like the Greene's home. Not like Charlotte.

I shook my head, hoping that would make the memories of the last few days go away, but I was kidding myself.

I fanned the lapels of my coat and mussed my hair. Subtle notes of vanilla drifted from my coat, and I suddenly felt the need for a long, long nap.

CHARLOTTE

"And," I said, taking a sharp breath, "That's how Opal became Roxanne, and how I am sitting here dying a little inside."

Bunny only blinked. Aunt Janice did the same.

I threw my hands in the air, "Say something!"

Bunny brought her fist to her mouth and cleared her throat. "Janice, darling. Could you give us a moment?" Janice slowly stood, and walked toward the kitchen.

"I," Bunny said, and I clenched my fists and set my jaw, "have been a terrible mother." My head jerked involuntarily, and I felt a canyon-sized line draw between my brows. "Say what now?"

"I had no idea," she sniffled, and pools began to form under her eyes, "I had no idea I was putting so much pressure on you."

"No, no, no," I fired in rapid succession, "You don't have to apologize."

"Of course, I do! The thought of potentially disappointing me led you to, well," she gestured around her, "this."

Aunt Janice appeared out of nowhere, slid a box of tissues to Bunny, and then slid back in the direction of the kitchen.

"This is not your fault." I grabbed Bunny's free hand as she dabbed a tissue at her cheeks with the other. "I chose to make things hard..." I sighed, released Bunny's hand, and cradled my face.

"Darling," she patted my knee, "all I've ever wanted from the pageants, the races, debate club, all of that nonsense," she flitted her hand in the air, "was for you to feel like you could do anything in the world you wanted to do. My childhood was very limited and had to find myself late in life. I did not want that for you, and if I was never clear about that, then I need to apologize."

"I'm sorry too," I wailed and flung my arms around my mom, and we sniffled and cried into each other's hair. When we released each other from the sob fest, dad was standing in front of us with his hands stuffed deep into his pockets, rocking from heel to toe.

"I made hot sandwiches," he whispered, "and the new Roxanne looks frightened."

Bunny cleared her throat, "Lewis, darling. Can you and Janice join me upstairs for a moment? I think we should plan a cruise." She turned down the corners of her mouth and gave him a wink. Dad nodded and gave a hard wink back to her.

As he gathered Aunt Janice, Bunny leaned in and whispered, "Are you okay alone? I can stay close if you want moral support, darling?"

"Honestly, I want to go upstairs and hide. I am simultaneously embarrassed and pissed off. The last time I saw Roxanne, she had movers in our apartment..."

Bunny stiffened.

"Two guys were pushing my mattress down the hallway and-"

"Excuse me, darling," She held up a finger interrupting my train of speech, "She took your mattress?"

"Well, yeah. She said she bought it, but we actually bought it together, and-"

"Where did you sleep?"

"I slept in my reading chair, but only for one night. I came here right after-"

She shot up and straightened her flannel pajamas, "Excuse me, darling. Bunny wants blood."

My jaw dropped. Aunt Janice and Lewis moved briskly up the stairs as the clicking of Bunny's heels turned to a battle cry - war drums against the hardwood.

OPAL

*W*hen I opened my eyes, the sun had set. Despite the snow, there were small groups of people walking along the sidewalk and a line forming outside the little Mexican place on the corner.

I was fine before all of this. My spartan apartment. My dating life non-existent since my divorce. I had not felt lonely. I had just been alone.

It seems ridiculous to miss someone this much when you've only known them for a blip in the grand scheme of things...

I leaned against the wall near the window and watched as couples huddled in the flurries, and my phone vibrated in my pocket.

CHARLOTTE

*R*oxanne stood from the barstool as Bunny got closer. I had never seen fear in her eyes before. It was satisfying.

"Roxanne, is it?" Bunny extended a hand.

"Yes, Mrs. Greene. It's so nice to-"

Bunny took Roxanne's hand and squeezed. "You," she seethed, "owe my daughter an apology."

"Bunny, this isn't necessary," I interjected.

"The hell it isn't." She said, cupping her other hand around Roxanne's.

"Mrs. Greene, I mean no offense, but this isn't any of your business."

Bunny dropped Roxanne's hand and stamped her fists into her hips. Roxanne shook her hand a little bit to get the feeling back in her fingers.

"None my business, young lady?" She whispered, eyes wide.

"Bunny, don't you have a cruise to plan? Please?" I put on my best please-god-go-upstairs smile.

Bunny looked at me and back at Roxanne. "I'll be upstairs."

We stood there looking at each other until we could no longer hear the clicking of heels and heard the slamming of a door.

"Your mom seems...nice."

"What are you doing here?"

"I think I've made that pretty clear."

"I'm sorry, but I don't know what you think clear is. Half of my notifications on my phone are pictures you've posted in the last three days of you and "your girl" celebrating Christmas. It looks like you've had an entire relationship in the last three days with Rachel. There was even a picture of the two of you in the background of one of your pictures, so what the fuck is that about?"

"Calm down."

"Oh, she did not just tell her to calm down!" Aunt Janice's voice rang out in the distance.

"Here's what I think happened. Stop me if I'm wrong about any of this. You moved in with Rachel the day you moved out of our place, correct?"

"Yes."

"You have been living with her since and in fact, live with her now, correct?"

"I'm moving out tonight. She already knows-"

"I'm not done. You bought that ring in that box for her, didn't you? Maybe not an engagement ring for her, but a Christmas gift."

"Does that even matter?"

"YES!" My voice filled the house. I took a breath and held out my hand. "Give me the box." Roxanne looked at me, inquisitively. "Give me the box. If it's mine, give it to me." She palmed the box and said, "Well, this is not going at all how I imagined it."

"Before I open this," I sat the box on the kitchen island and pulled my phone out of my back pocket and scrolled. "This ring is going to be a cushion-cut, blue sapphire with tiny diamond accents around it."

Roxanne's face faded of all color.

"I know this because Rachel is wearing a pendant around her neck in this picture that your dumbass posted on social media not even a whole 72 hours ago."

I tossed the box up in the air. She caught it in one hand.

"What did you honestly think was going to happen when you came here with half of another girl's Christmas present?"

"It's a placeholder, babe." She whispered and came in closer to me. I could smell her pungent, spiced cologne. I didn't remember it smelling so manufactured. "Until we get back home and you can pick out the one you want."

She ran her hands over my jawbones, tangling her fingers in my hair, messing my loose bun. "I messed up," she whispered, "I know I did. I want to make it right."

I looked at her. Her puppy brown eyes burrowed into mine.

"Rex…"

"…Yeah, babe."

"What's my favorite color?"

"What?"

"What's my favorite color?" She furrowed her brows and looked me up and down. I was wearing blue flannel pajamas with pale pink and white plaid.

Ding.

"I don't know. Blue?"

"How long have we known each other?"

"About a year." She smiled and kissed my cheek. I pressed my hand to her chest and gently pushed her away.

"How do I take my coffee?" "I don't know. You always make the coffee. What is this? A test or something?"

"Go home, Rex. Where ever you think that is."

Ding.

"You can answer that," I said, "It's Rachel. She's made cookies for you." I held up my phone to show her the picture that Rachel posted. The caption read, "Sweets for my sweet. Hope your business trip went well, gorgeous."

"Are you with that girl?" She asked, shoving her hands into her coat pockets. I felt my eyes grow three sizes,

"You don't have the right to ask me that question."

"Yeah. That's what I thought." She pulled a rental car key out of pocket.

"Look, I'm willing to forget about it. You and that girl. Pearl or whatever her name was. I'm willing to pick up where we left off if you are."

"You literally have another girlfriend!"

"Whatever. This was a mistake."

"Yeah."

"I'll see you around."

"Yeah." A closed and locked the door behind her. I was still angry. Shaking all over.

Then, I remembered something. I opened the door and shouted, "You owe me three hundred and fifty dollars for the fucking mattress!"

CHARLOTTE

I couldn't be in the house anymore. I need to clear my head.

I slung on some muck boots and a heavy, fleece-lined coat, and followed the path from the back porch to the barn. The security lights were reflecting light off of glittery patches of leftover snow and ice.

I yanked hard at the hen statue and removed the key from the panel. I sped through to kick the heat on and grabbed a cream soda on the way back through.

I felt lonely and tired. I stretched out on the couch and pulled the throw from the back of the couch over my legs.

A pair of black leather gloves tumbled into my laps. I slid my hands into them, held them to my face, and freed the tears that I had been holding hostage all evening.

PHONE

*D*ing.
 You won't believe what's been happening around here since you left!

CHARLOTTE

I woke up to the sun on my face, and my hands still in Opal's gloves. I stretched and pulled on my muck boots and coat. I pushed my gloved hands into my pocket and braced myself for the cold morning air.

It had snowed again. Just enough to cover the green and brown patches that were showing. It was beautiful and clean. I felt guilty for walking through it and messing it up.

"Good morning, darling!" Bunny squeezed me and took my coat. Janice brought house shoes to the door for me, and dad silently smiled as the two ladies fawned over me. Bunny wrapped a Mexican blanket around my shoulders. She and Aunt Janice walked me to the den and sat me in front of the fireplace.

"So, what happened?" Aunt Janice asked, pouring a cup of coffee.

"Oh, I think you heard what happened."

"Yeah," she scrunched her face about, "we could hear the loud parts. Sorry."

"It's okay. At least this way I don't have to relive it.

Thanks, dad." I said as he put a plate of fresh strawberry slices and french toast on my lap.

"So, darling," Bunny moved across from me, sitting eagerly on the ottoman, "I was thinking you should stay here for another day or two."

"I can't. I already have a plane ticket, and I have to work tomorrow…"

"What about Opal?" Aunt Janice said.

"What about her?"

"Well, aren't you going to call her?"

"I can't. I don't have her number. She's not on social media. And, she left. If she had wanted to stay, she would have stayed. And I just, just," tears streamed down my cheek, "I just let her leave."

"Did you check the app?"

"I checked it all night and ten times already this morning. Nothing."

"Give her time, darling." Bunny wrapped an arm around me and hugged me close. "She needs time too."

CHARLOTTE

We spent the day watching movies and napping here and there. Bunny and Aunt Janice took to the dining room table to plan a New Year celebration that would rival every ugly sweater party they'd ever thrown. I swiped through photos of Tree Day.

The afternoon turned to evening fast. I stuffed Opal's gloves in my coat pocket and stacked my luggage by the door.

"Sweetie, I'm sorry. I'm not going to be able to take you after all." Aunt Janice said as she crossed from kitchen to living room.

"That's fine. I can get a Tag-A-Ride." I reached for my phone and made a silent wish.

"Will the original do?"

CHARLOTTE

I froze. I looked at my phone to see if I could see Opal's icon on the app. Was her voice coming from the app?

A warm hand touched my arm, and I turned in its direction.

"Hey." She said softly.

"Hey." I sighed. I dropped my phone into my pocket and pulled out her gloves. "You left these here."

"Yeah. That's why I'm here." She said, lifting the corner of her mouth.

"I'm so glad you're here." I stood on tiptoes and threw my arms around her. Her arms wrapped around me and pulled me to close. I could feel her heart beating against mine.

Her hand found my cheek, and her soft, warm lips found mine.

Awes and clapping sounds came from the entryway.

"My family is so weird. Privacy, you guys! Please!" I laughed.

Opal's cheeks turned pink, and she pressed one against mine.

"Can we talk?" She whispered in my ear.
"Yes, please! I'd love to talk!"

OPAL

"Wow." It seemed too absurd to be true, but it was.

"Wow, indeed."

"She hadn't told the other girl, what's her name again?"

"Rachel."

"She hadn't told Rachel anything about coming to see you?"

"Nope."

"And, the ring was part of a set for Rachel?"

"Oh, yeah."

"Wow."

"Yeah."

"Blue sapphire? On what planet did she think she'd be able to pass off a blue sapphire anything as a gift she'd picked out especially for you?"

Charlotte chuckled and sipped her hot chocolate. Then, she looked at me and raised an eyebrow.

"Do I not seem like a blue sapphire kind of girl?"

"No."

"Interesting." She raised an eyebrow at me. She was

asking me to elaborate, but how could tell her that I knew I'd be giving her a diamond someday.

"We should get going if you're going to make your flight."

"I see what you did there. We aren't finished with that conversation, ma'am."

We made our way to the door and hugged everyone. I helped Charlotte into her coat and reached for the door.

"Wait!" She reached into my back pocket and took my phone. She tapped the screen a few times and held the screen up for me to see. "There. Now, you can call me."

"What if I don't want to call you? What if I want to see you?"

A grin swept across her face, and her cheeks turned an intense pink. "Well, we can arrange that."

"Magic." I pocketed my phone and opened the door. A cold breeze hit our faces. An icy breeze.

"Oh, my word." Bunny hugged herself and watched sheets of snow fell around the steps and my SUV.

"You don't happen to have the gym bag, do you?" Charlotte grinned.

"Yep." I smiled and kissed her cheek. "I'll be right back."

"Sandwiches?" Lewis asked.

"Oh, that sounds good. And soup. We need some soup." Janice said, following Lewis to the kitchen.

"Opal, darling! Hurry inside, dear! I'll pour us some wine, and you teach me to make an app!" Bunny shouted and waved her inside.

CHARLOTTE

ONE YEAR LATER

"*D*arling, your antlers are drooping!" Bunny adjusted the fuzzy, white antlers on my ugly Christmas sweater.

Opal chuckled and sipped eggnog from a moose shaped mug while Lewis played photographer.

"Why don't you ever take these pictures?" Opal asked Aunt Janice.

"Bunny insists that I am on vacation. I am to relax while she plays with my thousands of dollars of photo equipment. It's actually that she just wants to play with my toys like she did when we were little girls." She giggled, and I saw Opal cover her mouth and whisper in Aunt Janice's ear. Aunt Janice looked surprised, and she reached for her camera.

"What was that all about?" I asked Opal as we readied ourselves for the traditional ugly sweater photo.

"I just reminded her how much spiking of the eggnog Bunny had actually done before drinking her third glass.

"Darlings! Antlers!" Bunny said, holding up a moose mug of her own.

Aunt Janice was perched behind her camera. "Smile, ladies." She sang.

I pressed my back against Opal, and she wrapped her arms around me. We cheesed and made silly faces at the camera.

"One more, darlings. Mistletoe!" Bunny chirped.

"This will never end if we don't..." I turned to face Opal and found her kneeling with a small, pink box. "Oh, my god."

"Charlotte Greene with an E whose favorite color is pink. Who takes a little coffee with her cream. Who sings Motown in the shower. Who gives my life meaning, and who I love more and more each day," her hands were shaking as she cracked open the box, " Will you marry me?"

Tears were streaming down my cheeks and blurring my vision. I could see through the fog a simple emerald cut diamond set in white gold.

"Yes, of course. Yes, yes, yes." I wiped at my tears as she slid the ring onto my finger.

She pulled me close and kissed my forehead. "I love you, Charlotte."

"I love you, Opal."

"Oh, my darlings!" Bunny clicked to our sides and wrapped her arms around us. "I'm so happy for you both! I can think of only one thing that would make me happier than I am at this moment."

"Mom, don't!"

"Grandchildren!"

PHONE

Ding. Charlotte Greene and Opal Blackwood got engaged!

THE END

AUTHOR'S NOTE

Thank you so much for reading this very first novelette!

When I was in my early 20s, I was in my first serious relationship with a woman, and I wanted so badly to read about real, healthy, and good relationships between women. All I found were books about drugs, alcohol, and abuse of all kinds. It seemed that everyone's love was fraught with drama and pain.

I wanted a "candy bar" book. A book that was sweet and quick to read. I promised myself that I would make those books for others like me. And, here, right now in your hands, is the first of many books showcasing all kinds of love.

If you enjoyed this novelette, I hope you will tell your friends and visit my page on PilgrimFowlPress.com. You visit can also visit http://eepurl.com/gQPxZ1 to join my newsletter and never miss a new romance.

Thank you again!

Thank you to Unsplash.com and Thibault Debaene for the beautiful cover image.

Thank you also to my family and friends for understanding that locking myself in the bedroom with my computer is part of the job. I love you all more than coffee. That's a big deal.